D1130376

Illustrated by the Disney Storybook Artists

© 2008 Disney Enterprises, Inc.
This publication may not be reproduced in whole or in part by any means whatsoever without written permission from the copyright owners. Permission is never granted for commercial purposes.

Published by
Louis Weber, C.E.O.
Publications International, Ltd.
7373 North Cicero Avenue, Lincolnwood, Illinois 60712

Ground Floor, 59 Gloucester Place, London W1U 8JJ

Customer Service: 1-800-595-8484 or customer_service@pilbooks.com

www.pilbooks.com

p i kids is a registered trademark of Publications International, Ltd.

ISBN-13: 978-1-4127-6545-9
ISBN-10: 1-4127-6545-5

Belle was a beautiful girl who lived in a small village with her father, Maurice. Every day was exactly the same. She felt out of place in the quiet little town. Belle wanted a life full of excitement and adventure.

One morning, Belle went to read a book by a fountain. The local brute, Gaston, watched her walk down the street. All the women in the village adored Gaston and wanted to marry him. They thought he was handsome and strong. Belle thought he was conceited and rude.

"Only she is beautiful as me," said Gaston. "So I'm making plans to marry Belle!"

"Hello, Belle," Gaston said as he took her book.
"How can you read this? There's no pictures."

Belle grabbed her book.

"It's about time you got your head out of those books and paid attention to more important things," Gaston said. "Like me."

When Belle returned home, she expected her father, Maurice, to have returned from the inventors fair. But such was not the case. Only Phillipe, Maurice's horse, had returned. Belle's father was nowhere to be seen.

Belle raced back to where Phillipe had left Maurice and found a huge castle. Belle pushed open the castle door.

"Hello? Is anyone here? Papa?" Belle asked.

Belle found her father locked in the dungeon.

"Leave," Maurice warned. "You must go now!"

Suddenly the Beast appeared.

"Who's there?" Belle asked.

"The master of this castle," the Beast answered.

"I've come for my father. Please let him out," Belle begged. "Can't you see he's sick? Please. I'll do anything."

"There is nothing you can do," the Beast said.

"Wait," Belle said. "Take me instead."

"You would take his place?" the Beast asked.

Belle nodded. "You have my word."

The Beast did not make Belle stay in the dark cell. He took her to her own room.

"The castle is your home now," the Beast said. "You can go anywhere you like, except the west wing. It is forbidden."

Belle was all alone in her room. She started to cry. Then there was a soft knock on her door.

"I thought you might like a spot of tea," said Mrs. Potts, the teapot. "Cheer up, child," Mrs. Potts said. "It will turn out all right in the end. You'll see."

That night, the Beast waited and waited for Belle to join him for dinner. He grew very impatient.

"I told her to come down," he roared. "Why isn't she here yet?"

"Oh, try to be patient, sir," Mrs. Potts said.

Everyone hoped that Belle would fall in love with the Beast and break the spell they were under.

Late that night, Belle went downstairs. She ran into Lumiere, an enchanted candlestick, and Cogsworth, an enchanted clock.

"I am a little hungry," she told her new friends.

"Break out the silver," Mrs. Potts said. "Wake the china!" Soon all the dishes were singing and dancing. Belle liked her new friends. They made her feel at home.

After dinner, Belle sneaked into the west wing.
There she saw a single red rose under glass. Before she
could touch it, the Beast jumped in front of her.

"I warned you never to come here," the
Beast yelled. Frightened, Belle decided she
couldn't stay at the castle any longer.
She rushed into the forest and was
surrounded by wolves. The
Beast came to Belle's
rescue just in time.

Over time, Belle started to feel at home in the castle. She even began to look forward to spending time with the Beast each day.

They spent hours reading stories. They even played in the snow. Belle taught the Beast how to feed the tiny birds that lived on the castle grounds.

The Beast wanted to give Belle a present. He told her to close her eyes and led her to the castle's library.

Belle opened her eyes and gasped. She had never seen so many books in her life. It was the best gift anyone had ever given her.

Later that night, Belle and the Beast ate dinner together. They danced, just like a prince and princess.

"Belle, are you happy here with me?" the Beast asked.
Belle said yes, but hesitated. She was beginning to
care deeply for the Beast, but she also missed her father.

"If only I could see my father again," Belle said.

The Beast understood. He showed Belle his magic
mirror. She looked into the mirror and saw her father. He
was sick and alone.

The Beast could tell that Belle was worried about her father. He also knew that if Belle left the castle, the spell might never be broken and he would remain a Beast forever. But he loved Belle and wanted her to be happy.

"You must go to him," the Beast said. He gave Belle the mirror so she would always remember him.

"Thank you," Belle said before leaving.

"How did you escape?" Maurice asked Belle when she returned.

"He's different now," Belle said. "He's changed somehow." Belle already missed the Beast.

Knock, knock, knock! Someone pounded on the door.

"I've come to collect your father," a man told Belle.

"My father is not crazy," Belle told the crowd gathered outside the house.

"I might be able to clear up this misunderstanding if you marry me," said Gaston.

"Never!" Belle cried. She ran to get the magic mirror.

"My father is not crazy and I can prove it." Belle showed the townspeople the Beast.

"Is he dangerous?" asked one of the townspeople.

"He would never hurt anyone," Belle said.

"Follow me!" Gaston shouted. He and the
townspeople marched to the Beast's castle.

The Beast refused to fight, but when he saw Belle,
his heart soared. The Beast reached for Belle's hand,
but Gaston wounded him. Gaston fell to the ground.

Belle gasped and ran to the Beast.

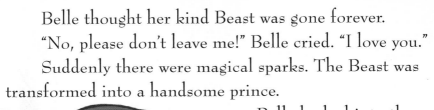

Belle thought her kind Beast was gone forever.
"No, please don't leave me!" Belle cried. "I love you."
Suddenly there were magical sparks. The Beast was
transformed into a handsome prince.

Belle looked into the
prince's eyes. She saw that
they were the same kind,
blue eyes. Because Belle
had seen the true beauty
inside the Beast, the spell
was broken.